P9-BYK-968

I Like School

from the library of

by Michaela Muntean
Illustrated by Tom Herbert

Featuring Jim Henson's Sesame Street Muppets

A SESAME STREET/GOLDEN PRESS BOOK
Published by Western Publishing Company, Inc.
in conjunction with Children's Television Workshop.

© 1980 Children's Television Workshop. Muppet characters
© 1980 Muppets, Inc. All rights reserved. Printed in U.S.A.
SESAME STREET®, the SESAME STREET SIGN, and SESAME STREET BOOK CLUB
are trademarks and service marks of Children's Television Workshop.
GOLDEN® and GOLDEN PRESS® are trademarks of Western Publishing Company, Inc.
No part of this book may be reproduced or copied in any form
without written permission from the publisher.
Library of Congress Catalog Card Number: 80-50236
ISBN 0-307-23111-9

flag

STO[P]

bus

slide

playgroun[d]

lunch
box

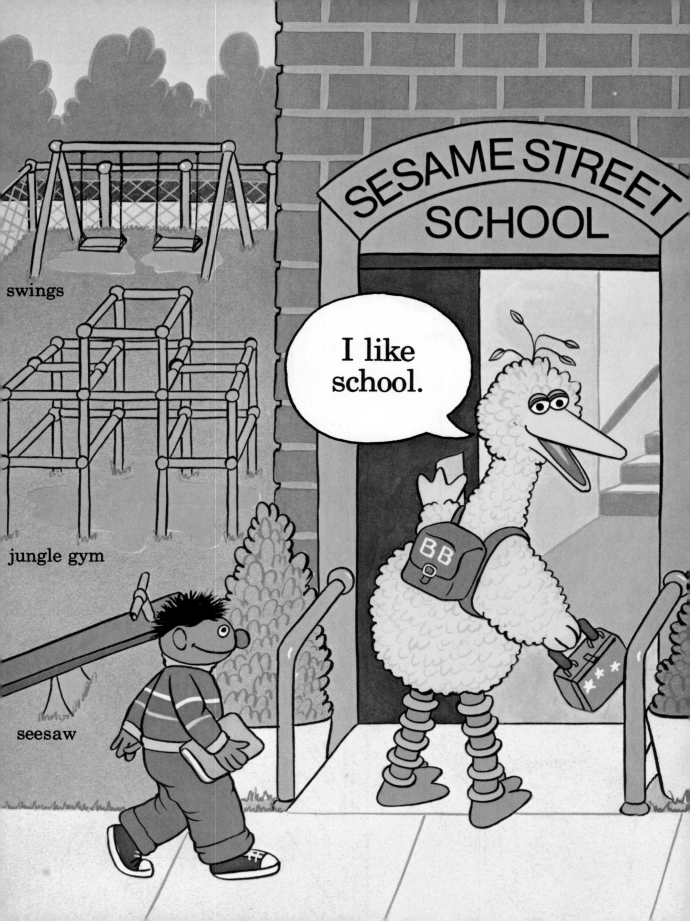

swings

jungle gym

seesaw

ABCDEFGHIJKLM

chalkboard

NOPQRSTUVWXYZ

alphabet

clock

BERT
BERT
BERT
BERT

chalk

eraser

book cart

bookshelf

librarian

library card

book stamp

books

CHECK BOOKS OUT HERE

RETURN BOOKS HERE

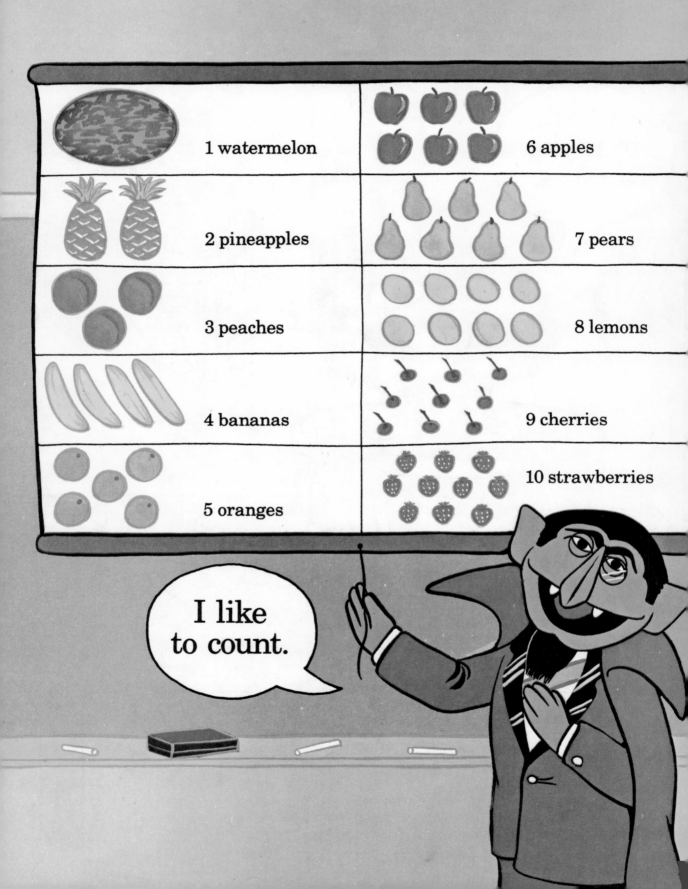

raisins

plates

carrots

nuts

triangle

music book

piano

cymbals

jump rope

swing

seesaw

ball

After school, I like to ride home on the school bus.

seat

driver

steering wheel

HISTORY OF TRASH

ABCDEFGHIJ